CHUCK NASTY PRESENTS: EROTIC GORE

Chuck Nasty

Unveiling Nightmares Ltd

Book Cover by Christy Aldridge Grim Poppy Designs

Editor Crystal Baynam

CONTENTS

Dedicated to the horror hosts that are out there introducing people to the films in the genre we all love. Most importantly, to Joe Bob Briggs for continuing to introduce myself and others to the many fucked up films that slipped through the cracks. The drive-in never dies!

INTRODUCTION

Hello there! If you are reading this, then that must mean you picked up a copy of this special little dirty double release. When the idea came about to put these two stories in one piece of literature, I was back and forth. However, it didn't take me too long to decide. I did, in fact, like the idea. Originally, this idea was to put out a double feature, like if you were going to the theater. After thinking more about it, I decided that going another route would make more sense.

Having a love for horror showcases with horror hosts. I wanted to put out something as a tribute to all those types of shows. My two favorite shows to watch as a kid were Monster Vision, hosted by Joe Bob Briggs and the Friday and Saturday night film raunch fest; USA Up All Night, hosted by the beautiful and goofy Rhonda Shear one night, while the late great, Gilbert Godfrey hosted whichever night that Rhonda didn't. I am pretty sure Rhonda hosted on Fridays and Gilbert on Saturdays. Either way, both were usually fun to watch. Monster Vision is where I would end up getting my weekly dose of gore, Up All Night is where I got my share of 80's teen sex comedies, but, sometimes, a horror film of some caliber would be shown.

One of the most important films I was shown on UAL was a not-so-great shlock feature titled: Sorority Girls and the Creature from Hell. When I wasn't able to stay up on the weekends and watch my favorite shows, I would set up my VCR with the timed record setting and would have it set to record all night or until the tape ran out; thus, how I discovered SGATCFH. It became a favorite film of mine as pre-teen. It had everything a growing boy wants in his films: bare breasts, blood, cheap gore...did I mention breasts?

During that time, I found myself being sucked into the *smut* being played over on USA Network. However, it was also the same time TNT started doing the Monster Vision show with Joe Bob. As I stated above, most of what I got from the USA was the goofy teen sex flicks that would have nude scenes that occasionally got past the censors. There were also moments when they would slap in either a B movie or a horror flick, or there would be rare occasions when they would have a good one in the mix. That's actually how I first saw the original Evil Dead (Thanks, Gilbert, RIP).

Monster Vision was the first horror showcase I saw that was on cable that was dedicated to the hardcore horror brought to us by the 70's, 80's and the 90's. My first time seeing, what I consider one of my favorite John Carpenter films, *The Fog*. Come to think of it, that may be the first time I came across Monster Vision late night channel surfing. As I get older it gets harder to remember some things, one thing I don't think I will ever forget is the way Joe Bob would say "The Fawg" in that strong southern accent of his. I would later meet the man himself (along with beautiful, Darcy the mail girl) which, I mentioned to him about my first time seeing The Fog. Sadly, I was intoxicated that evening and I am sure my words came out like a jumbled fart that's been stuck in the fat folds for hours, waiting for that certain moment where it's completely unacceptable to let one slip out. I am sure my words came out just like that. Either way, it was a complete honor to meet him and Miss Darcy. I also have to add, Joe Bob and Darcy still host The Last Drive-In on Shudder, keeping the drive-in alive (if you know, you know)! There isn't an episode I haven't watched. I highly recommend checking it out if you have not done so before reading this.

The two stories that were picked to be in this *double feature* are two stories that I feel are close to something I would see on a late-night horror showcase, maybe more fucked up than what can be shown on cable television, but you'll get what I mean after you take a gander through these pages. These are two of my favorites that I have written and published. Both stories are crude, rude and in your face with depravity and filth. Some things in these stories made me gag while writing them.

So, grab a six pack of your favorite brew, get the popcorn brewing and cannabis burning. It's time for CHUCK NASTY PRESENTS!

-CN

A SADOMASOCHISTIC ROMANCE

This first tale was written for the Unveiling Nightmare's anthology, Body Horror.

This was a fun story idea I wanted to mess with. Looking back on it, this story is about more than really meets the eye. Yes, there is deranged sex and unusual gore throughout this piece, but it's about so much more.

This is one where it's about many topics. There's love, acceptance, betrayal, finding oneself, etc. I don't want to give anything away in case your eyes haven't read this one yet.

I take great pride in this piece and have even considered expanding it into a larger project. However, whether this idea comes to fruition is a mystery for now, adding an element of anticipation for potential future works.

So, get ready to get hot and hard...A SADOMASOCHISTIC ROMANCE!

Everything was going as planned. With the money I'd saved for the last few years, I could find a cheap apartment in a bigger place with a warmer climate. Living my whole life in an area that always seemed to be gray and cold didn't help my growing depression.

Making friends didn't take as long as I figured it would. While attending a late-night showing of PSYCHO II at the local theater, I ran into a small group of people around my age. Two girls and two guys—couples. Their names weren't necessary. The only thing anyone needs to know is that one evening, after befriending this small group, one of the young women made a pass at me. I kindly declined. She was the type who always got what she wanted lest there be hell to pay; I was unaware of this fact beforehand. That's when I was confronted by her boyfriend, who didn't ask questions, just walked up and socked me a good one in the face. I tried to explain that nothing happened as she stood next to him, grinning ear to ear. Apparently, she told him I tried to kiss her and shove her face on my cock. These things, as I stated, did not happen.

After getting my ass handed to me by the rather large man, who used to play football and wrestle, it was time to start over. I had a tad bit of a fear that more bullshit would be started due to rumors and such. However, none of that ended up being an issue. My ass got beat, and I was left alone. This meant that I needed to find a new crowd. Maybe things would work better if I toned down the good guy act and took on a new personality.

One evening, after a few drinks at the bar a few blocks from my apartment, I met an interesting man and woman—a married couple a few years older than myself. I had never met anyone like Don and Jasmine Hopper.

While outside, having a quick smoke after downing a pint of beer and three shots, I was joined by the Hoppers. Don was the first to stumble onto the back patio, waving a beer above his head, laughing hysterically. He was ranting about something, but being so drunk, his words didn't make much sense as he walked over to me to bum a light for the half-broken cigarette dangling from his lips.

"You ever seen the inside of a horse's anus?" the spiked-haired man asked, holding his hand out, making a gesture that let me know he needed a lighter.

"Wha-huh?" I responded, handing him my little blue cheapy.

He laughed louder. "Never mind." He lit the cigarette, inhaled, and flipped the little switch on the lighter to increase the flame's height. I watched as he lifted his other arm and lowered it atop the fire. The sizzling of his arm hair and flesh produced an odor that immediately made me want to puke.

Jasmine ran up and wrapped her arms around Don's neck. Her laugh was as psychotic as his as she watched his flesh sizzle. The way he gnashed the cigarette filter with his teeth and how the sweat poured down his face, I could tell he was in pain.

"Oh baby, are you showing off again?" Jasmine asked, leaning into Don's ear. "Why do you always waste your anger on yourself when you have me?"

"Shit, Jas!" Don tossed the lighter back to me, which I caught clumsily and shoved into my pocket. He turned around and grabbed the woman by the face with both hands, kissing her on the lips.

I smiled awkwardly.

"What's your name?" Jasmine asked, looking past Don.

"Yeah, what's your name, bub?" There was something sinister about Don's half-grin; it should have been a red flag.

"Chase." I extended my hand to shake Don's.

He glanced down at my hand before reciprocating. Smoke rolled from his nostrils as he slightly shook his head, still grinning. As if things hadn't been odd enough, Jasmine ran up and pulled her thin crop top down, exposing her breasts and shaking them at me.

"Woah!" I said, turning my head away, not wanting to get my head knocked in by the crazy man.

"What's the matter, man? Not big enough for ya?" Don laughed, grabbing a handful of his wife's tit. "I find them to be quite perfect." He jokingly acted offended.

"I think he just doesn't want to be rude, baby!" The drunken Jasmine Hopper, chesticles still in the wind, ran to me with a big smile across her face. "Here, it's okay. Don is pretty proud of them." She laughed, holding a breast in each palm.

I shook my head. "No, that's fine. Really?" To be perfectly honest, I wanted to grab hold of them. They were nice. And not being the kind of guy who got laid much, I wanted to gobble them up. Jasmine grabbed my arm and raised my hand to her left tit. So, I squeezed.

"Whatcha' think, Chase?" Don inquired, stepping closer to me.

My first thought was to flinch, thinking a punch to the temple was about to happen. Nope. Don put his arm around my neck as if we were old buddies. He didn't seem angry; this confused me. "I mean, they are nice."

"Just nice?" Jasmine bit her bottom lip, giving her tits a wobble, while I took in the feeling of holding onto one of them.

"Now, let's not offend the wife here, Chase. Tell her how you really feel about those fun bags!" Don excitedly demanded.

What was I supposed to do? "I think they are fucking amazing," I answered, mumbling just enough for them to hear me. They laughed. Don, still having his arm around my neck, gave me a nudge. My hand automatically fell from the breast.

"Come on, Chase! You seem to be a pretty good dude. I'm a good judge of character. Let's go have some drinks. On us!" Then Don paused. "How rude of us! I'm Don Hopper, and that's my wife, Jasmine."

"Let me put the girls away." Jasmine giggled, pulling her crop top back over her chest. Don walked around to the other side of her. She quickly slid her arm under his, then looped my arm with her free arm as we walked back into the bar.

I didn't spend a dime on a drink for the rest of the evening. The Hoppers seemed well-off, tipping the bartender a twenty for every other drink he bought. It would be a good guess to say he probably spent over a thousand dollars in less than three hours.

Even though the Hoppers didn't act very civilized in public, their company was a breath of fresh air. The whole rest of the evening was full of strange conversations having to do with everything from lizard people to what we all thought Dolly Pardon's tits looked like at her age. There were a few moments where I ended up seeing more of both Don and Jasmine. Don would be talking very passionately about the homeless crisis in America, all the while spreading his wife's legs, pushing her skirt to the side, and sliding his fingers in and out of her shaved nether region like it was nothing. Not long after, Jasmine released Don's rather large member from his pants and violently jammed it down her throat. Keep in mind we were sitting at the bar.

When the bartender kicked us out, Don and Jasmine complained that it was too early for the evening to end. I had such a drunkenly fun time that I didn't want it to end either. The night had been weird, but in a good way, and curiosity made me want to tag along with them further. When they asked, I replied with a hardy "Sure!"

Before my journey of starting over, the craziest things I had ever been guilty of were being a pushover and a stick in the mud, never just going with the flow of life and letting things happen when they should. Paranoia was another issue that kept me from being able to have any damn fun. I have to thank these two for opening my mind. With that said, their influence became unhealthy.

It seemed like Don and Jasmine were around every day. Either they would be knocking on my door, waking me up to go drinking with them, which usually ended up with me trying whatever narcotic those two were sportin' that day, or we would rotate whose place we crashed at after the high wore off. Honestly, life became a blur. Time seemed to speed up.

There may have been a nice chunk of change in my savings account. It would run out sooner than later if I didn't get a job. Don and Jasmine weren't worried about me finding a place of employment. Don told me as long as we all kept hanging out, I wouldn't need to worry about anything in the cash department. This resulted in my moving into their house. It may seem strange to say, but both of them made me nervous. The hedonistic nature of how they lived appealed to me; my whole life was pretty fucking boring, and they were the right people to bring out my wild side. Every day, I was curious about what would come next.

Curiosity killed the cat.

One night, after returning from a night of drinking, all three of us fell into the door, piling up on each other, laughing like drunken banshees. Jasmine was the first to get up from the marble floor. She ran to the little bar a few feet from the front door. "Who's thirsty?" she hollered, already pouring a brown liquid into three crystal clear drinking glasses.

"I would love that!" Don exhaustingly shouted back. He reached down and helped me to my feet. "You wanna drink?" he asked.

"Yeah, sure, why not?" I replied.

Jasmine walked around the bar to bring us our drinks. She was always so chipper and happy, no matter the situation. Her enthusiasm was refreshing as well as motivating. When she handed me one of the glasses of whiskey, she stood on her toes and kissed my forehead, giggling. She walked over to Don. When she handed him his glass, he chugged the contents and set the glass down on a table. He grabbed Jasmine around the waist and pulled her closer, smashing his lips down on hers. They locked in an embrace. Then Jasmine slid her skirt off, revealing she wasn't wearing any panties, which seemed to be a trend with her.

Don caressed between her legs as she removed her top. What was I doing? Standing there in disbelief.

A part of me imagined some weird sex act happening between the three of us at some point, but this caught me off guard. Don picked Jasmine up by the ass, lifting her onto the bar. The spotlights above the bar shined down onto Jasmine's naked body, illuminating her many scars. I had never noticed them before, but to be honest, we stayed fucked up every night and slept all day. When would I have paid that much attention?

"Come here, Chase!" Don waved me over.

"Why?" A snicker came out with my words.

Don glared at me. "Don't be afraid. I want you to come here and put your tongue inside my wife. I need to do something."

"Excuse me?" I wasn't sure I heard him correctly.

Don stomped over and grabbed my shirt, yanking me over to where Jasmine was leaning back on the bar, propping herself up by her elbows and spreading her legs while her giant tits hung slightly to the sides.

"Just eat her goddamn pussy, boy!" Don demanded with a grin stretching across his face.

I could see no other option than to do as I was told. Honestly, I didn't mind having to perform such a task. It was just the first time there had ever been more than me and one other person in the room—and the third person in this scenario was the husband of the woman sprawled out naked in front of me.

Doing as told, I sat on a bar stool in front of Jasmine. Her pussy looked so smooth and was about the only part of her I could see that wasn't scarred up. Without hesitation, I eased my mouth closer to her holiest of holies, flicking my tongue on her clit. Jasmine moaned.

"That feels so good, Chase!" She reached over and aggressively grasped Don's shirt. "Cut me!" she screamed in his face.

Part of me ignored what she said, while the other part was concerned about what would happen. I considered her scars and decided there wasn't much need for worry. It was apparent they did that kind of thing a lot. I kept licking away, and as I did, the shakier Jasmine became. Her body had moments of twitching, which told me I was doing something right. My confidence was soaring. I moved my tongue down, sliding it as deep as I could, bobbing my head back and forth, tongue-fucking her dripping hole.

"Oh my God!" Jasmine suddenly started screaming. It startled me, and I quickly lifted my head from her dripping crotch. To my horror, Don was taking a long knife and slicing her breasts. Blood dribbled from her chest, trickling down to the area I had been licking. Crimson slowly covered her clitoris. "Lick it." Jasmine moaned.

As I stared into her eyes, I lowered my head, running my tongue up her slit to her bellybutton, tasting the red warmth. I swallowed. Don and Jasmine both watched with pleasure as I found myself lapping up her blood. My tongue continued up Jasmine's torso, swallowing the red as I went. When my mouth reached between her breasts, my first instinct was to kiss over her heart.

"Look at that, baby. Seems like Chase is enjoying himself." Don pushed his face against Jasmine's cheek, kissing her gently. "How about some more?" He shouted, taking the blade and making more incisions into her skin. Like an artist at work, he waved the knife, making strokes as if he were holding a paintbrush.

While blood splattered and misted across my face, my eyes wouldn't close, and my head wouldn't turn away. I was mesmerized. Jasmine was on her back, hanging her head backwards behind the counter. I thought she was dead. Then I heard laughing.

Don stood beside her, one hand gripping the knife, the other reaching down. He grabbed a handful of Jasmine's hair and lifted it. Although her face looked like it had gone through a blood bukkake and her eye shadow was making trails down her face, she was the one who was laughing.

I stood and backed up slowly, heading to the front door. They both stared at me, laughing hysterically. Catching a glimpse of myself in a hallway mirror, I was covered from my head down in red. "Shit," I mumbled.

"Don't leave, Chasey boy! She's fine. Sure, she's a mess at the moment, but it's just part of our lifestyle." Don's voice became calm. "Look, if you really want to head out, that's fine. I'm not really sure where you plan on going, but you might want to shower first."

"Yeah, all that blood may have cops lookin' at you weird," Jasmine chimed in, hopping off the bar, chunks of her flesh falling to the floor. During the excitement, I hadn't noticed the severity of the slashing Don had given her with the sharp blade. She limped over to where I stood.

Too freaked out to move, my eyes followed her. "What the fuck is going on? Aren't you in pain?" Nothing else seemed appropriate to blurt out. I glanced over at Don, who was cleaning his knife at the sink behind the bar. I shook my head in disbelief.

"Fuck yeah! It hurts a lot." Jasmine raised her arms, and more skin slices dripped off, splatting to the floor.

"How the hell are you not in excruciating pain? Your skin is literally on the floor, looking like thin slices of lunch meat! What the fuck is going on?" I realized my tone had gotten louder, so I quickly took it down a notch, fearing it might anger Don.

"It stings a lot, but the real pain doesn't last long. It grows back in no time," Don said, staring in my direction and drying his hands with a white towel.

"Yeah, it only hurts for a bit. We like the pain to be pretty brutal!" Jasmine sensually ran her hands up and down her belly, up to her breast, moaning.

"I don't understand. You like being sliced open like that?" I asked.

"Baby, you haven't lived until you can understand the orgasm I get when it comes to my threshold of pain. When Don abuses me, it's just foreplay." She laughed.

What a weird statement to make. When I first started hanging out with Don and Jasmine, I already knew they were a little on the crazy side. Hell, that was a huge reason I liked being around them. They were different from the fuckers back home who did nothing but stay home and play video games. I needed some adventure. Mission: accomplished. However, this situation I had willingly placed myself in had taken a dark turn, and all I wanted to do was go the fuck home. But seeing as I was covered in a woman's blood, there was no choice but to walk my happy ass up the stairs and get into the shower.

Don stopped me.

"What? That's it? Just gonna take a shower and leave us?" Don stood nose to nose with me. I could feel his heavy breathing on my face. His teeth were gritting. This is where I sensed a punch to the face coming—sensed piss about to go down my leg, too.

Everything went silent. The tension in the room had my body shaking. I stared into Don's eyes; I swear there were flames. Then he laughed, and Jasmine joined him. Her laugh was louder, higher pitched, and frankly, frightening.

"He's just fucking with you, Chase. Go take a shower, and when you're done, we will answer any questions you might have," Jasmine said, her voice becoming softer and more caring.

"Yeah, no worries, bub. The way you are acting is perfectly normal." Don backed up from my personal space and placed his hands on my shoulders like a dad would do in an old sitcom before explaining the wrongs and rights of the world. "There are a lot of things we haven't told you. I guess tonight is the night you find out about everything."

I stood there looking at him like a scolded child.

"Seriously, it's going to be fine. Go shower. Jasmine and I will prepare some grub for when you're done."

Without speaking a word, I directed myself to the stairs. For whatever reason, I looked back at Don and Jasmine. They were embracing each other. In the quiet of the moment, I could hear Jasmine's blood squish as she rubbed against Don's sleeveless shirt. They paid me no mind.

⸻☠⸻

While scrubbing the blood off myself, I suddenly began weeping. I was scared to shit. My mind raced. One second, images of my old life flashed through my head, and then I thought about the dumb decisions I'd made since the Hoppers came into my life.

The water felt like it had cleansed my skin, and after a good cry, I calmed myself down. When I stepped out of the shower, I looked down at my pile of bloody clothes. Realizing I forgot to grab clean clothes from my room before hopping in the shower, I wrapped a towel around myself and walked into the hallway. There was silence, not even a TV on or even them talking to each other. Looking at my closed bedroom door a couple of doors down, I sighed and went in the other direction, down the steps.

"Don? Jasmine?" I called out while creeping down the stairs.

No answer.

A big part of me wanted to get back up the stairs, dive into my room, gather as much as possible, and load my car down. Unfortunately, I tend to be a bit of a glutton for punishment. Mix that with a curious mind, and it can get toxic.

"You all down here?" I shouted out, hoping for a reply. "If you all are playing one of your sick fucking games—" My words were cut off. A sound came from the living room. Hesitantly, I walked to the open room. It was pitch black. "Guys?"

Suddenly, something pulled the towel away from me, exposing my naked body to the darkness. I heard whatever it was scurry away from me. The faint sound of snickering echoed in the dark, as well.

A red light came on overhead, lighting the room in a crimson glow. I thought things couldn't get much worse. I should have known I was lying to myself. When the light came on, it revealed Don and Jasmine Hopper sprawled across the floor—in pieces.

Chunks of flesh were stuck against the walls, and arms and legs were strewn from one side of the room to the next. Most disturbing was how Don and Jasmine stared at me from the floor in front of the fireplace. With only his head and one arm attached, Don's torso seemed to wave at me. Jasmine was in a similar state, but both arms were attached. Her legs were missing. She also appeared to be waving. Maniacal grins stretched across both of their faces.

I felt dizzy. The room started to spin. The last things I remember before I blacked out were images of Don using a knife to slice open Jasmine's stomach with her tit in his mouth. As my body fell toward the floor, the last image was of Don pulling Jasmine's insides from her gut and playing around in her innards while Jasmine used a knife to saw off his penis. They both cackled like banshees.

⚊⚊☠⚊⚊

When I finally woke up, it wasn't on my own. Jasmine was poking my forehead with her middle finger. It took me a second to recall the details of the night before. My eyes opened, and I was thrilled to see Jasmine Hopper bent over me. I sunk back into the couch, not quite sure what to believe. Had I dreamed everything?

"Morning, silly. Crazy night last night, huh?" she asked, adding a cute little giggle as she spoke. She looked great. It had been months since I moved in with them on a whim, and I never thought she was that hot. I never thought she was ugly, either; I guess she just wasn't my type. But that morning, she looked radiant. She looked like she had just stepped out of the shower. Her hair was still wet. Although she wasn't fully naked, her petite silk robe showed me that more scars had popped up on her body. Fresh-looking scars wrapped around her legs in two places.

"What the hell is going on here, Jasmine?" I inquired aggressively, sitting up. My head had a knot from where I fell.

Jasmine sighed and sat next to me. "Look, we know you are kind of freaked out."

"Kinda?"

"Okay, so you are really fucking freaked out. We get it. But you need to know that we like you. That's why we are showing you these things now. We picked up on it when we met you at the bar that night." She placed a hand on my knee. I was still naked, but apparently, they covered me with a blanket while I slept. "You have potential, honey."

"What did you pick up on? Potential for what? I don't know what the fuck is going on! I saw you in pieces all over this fucking room!" There was a lot to take in. My confusion and disbelief were in a head-to-head battle to see which would drive me fucking insane first.

She smiled and leaned over, pressing her lips against mine. "It's still early. Why don't you go to your room and get some more sleep? Don and I have something special planned."

I felt plenty confident that whatever they had planned was most likely going to be fucking weird. However, I was okay with that.

Jasmine stood and walked in the direction of the kitchen. Taking her advice, I got up as well. The blanket fell to the floor. Looking down at the morning wood I was sporting, I decided to visit the restroom to take a piss before getting more rest. I grabbed the blanket, wrapped it around my waist, darted out of the living room, and leapt up the stairs as quickly as possible.

The sleep was well-needed. It lasted only a few hours but was a good power nap. My energy was back, and the hangover was nearly gone. As a newbie to the Hoppers' world, I became fascinated with drugs and alcohol like a child tasting candy for the first time. After spending as much time as I had with those two, it became painfully evident that pleasure had never been a significant part of my life. Sure, I enjoyed stuff and had fun, but never the kind of fun the Hoppers enjoyed.

Groggy as shit, I wandered down the stairs, only wearing pair of basketball shorts and a plain black shirt. The lights were dim, and the curtains were placed over the windows. Don sat at the end of the long table in the dining room. He stood up and threw something my way. I caught it. It was a cold Coors Light. Shrugging, I pulled the tab and chugged half the can in three gulps.

Don laughed. "Good catch!" he hollered, waving me to come closer. A laptop computer sat on the edge of the table. "I wanna' show you something!" He seemed very dialed in on whatever was on the screen.

"What's that?" I dragged my feet as I walked closer to him.

His sinister grin had returned and covered the bottom half of his face. "I want you to watch this video I found." Don leaned back in his chair and set his feet on the table.

I walked around to see what was so damn amazing. "Don, what am I looking at?" I asked.

Don pushed the play button as soon as I could see the screen. Without saying a word, he stared at me, waiting for my reaction.

The audio of screams played over a blank screen. Seconds later, a close-up image of a woman's mouth appeared. Slowly, the camera zoomed out, revealing more of the scene. The woman was screaming. Tears were running down her face. Little by little, more of the image came into the frame. The woman's left arm had been hacked off, while her right hand held a knife. I watched as she began stabbing herself in the torso, over and over. With each jab, blood spurted out, spraying over the woman's mangled body. By that point, her crying turned to laughing. The camera zoomed out more. Now I could see the woman was missing a leg. It was easier to see the multiple slash marks littering her flesh.

The video went blank, cutting to the next scene. This time, when the video continued to play, the same woman was lying in pieces all over the bed. But she was still alive. Her cries became screams of pain. A man's voice in the background kept repeating, "That's it. That's it. Wait for it." Then it went silent. The mangled woman stopped screaming. Her eyes went blank.

"Keep watching. It's not done yet." Don could tell that I wasn't too pleased. Hell, I probably looked downright terrified. My brain could only handle so much. Now I was watching this smut video with Don. I remembered the images from when I passed out the previous evening. He and Jasmine had both been cut to pieces, just like the woman in the video.

"What am I waiting for, Don? I'm still fucked up over last night. What the fuck was that?" Wanting answers, I looked away from the screen and glanced at Don.

He pointed at the screen.

The mutilated woman suddenly started flopping around on the bed. Her mouth draped open; blood poured out. The flesh flayed from her bones was beginning to grow back. The camera view focused on one of her bloody arm stumps. It split open as something broke through the surface of her skin. Fingers poked through as they extended outward. Before I knew it, a hand was growing from the wound. Then, it was an entire arm. The woman's limbs were growing back!

I could feel my heart about to burst through my chest. Sweat poured down my head. Was I having a heart attack? Nope—a panic attack. My eyes rolled into the back of my head, and my face smashed into the table. I was out like a light on the floor. It was becoming an annoying issue, not to mention slightly embarrassing.

※

"Wakey, wakey," Don said into my ear while smacking me and then throwing water on my face. I was no longer on the floor. I was sitting in the chair he had been using. The ice-cold water made my eyes fly open and my body jerk. Wiping the water from my eyes, I was astounded at what was in front of me on the long, conference-style table. It was Jasmine. She was lying flat with her legs spread. "Glad you are awake, Bud! It's time to have some fun."

"Fun? I am really starting to wonder about what you all consider fun!" I snapped.

"Calm down! Things are not as bad as you may think," Don said, patting me on the shoulder.

Jasmine took her hands and scooted her naked body around. Still lying on her back, she looked up at me and smiled. "You're a skittish one, aren't ya'?" she asked, rubbing her fingernails up and down her midsection. "There's nothing to worry about. I promise."

"Nothing to worry about? Since I started hanging out with you all, I have managed to become a heavy drinker, a cigarette smoker, and a drug taker. Then I walked downstairs to see blood everywhere, body parts flung on each side of the living room—your body parts! Then I wake up, and everything seems normal!" Frantically, I stood up from the chair, attempting to remove myself.

Don stopped me. His hand was still on my shoulder. All he had to do was push down, and I followed, plopping back into the chair.

"Will someone explain what the fuck is going on here?" I implored.

Don looked down at Jasmine, who sighed and sat up. She crossed her legs and sat "Indiana style" in front of me on the table. One of her hands reached out and gently rubbed my face. "Darlin', you need to listen and listen good."

My eyes must've looked like they were spasming. I kept finding myself focusing my attention on her beautifully large breasts.

"Usually, I would say look at them and even feel free to put them in your mouth," she continued. "This, however, is a time you need to listen the fuck up. Don't want to miss any details, do ya?"

My attention was at its peak. Leaning back in my chair, I focused. My ears were ready to listen.

She began:

"We haven't always been this way. It just kind of happened. Don and I were two fuckups who stayed fucked up all the time. The only things that kept our interest were drugs, alcohol, and kinky sex." She spoke softly as she caressed her breasts with both hands.

"When I say kinky, I mean kinky! It started with me submitting to Don and then him submitting to me. The usual penetration from his penis was great, and I still adore choking on that hog. But I need something more. As a teen, self-mutilation became a ritual in my everyday life. A little cut here, a few burns there. The pain made me wet." She was clearly getting excited while reminiscing. She scooted back on the table and propped her legs up with knees in the air.

While rubbing her clitoris, she continued. "So, many years later, as Don and I were trying new ways to make each other come, I recalled my youth. I thought, maybe some extra pain is what we needed for the maximum orgasm!" she slid her fingers in and out of the sweet pink between her thighs. "We incorporated cutting into our sex play. It started with simple little gashes here and there while Don pounded my guts with that big meat stick of his."

From the side of my eye, I noticed that Don had pulled said meat stick from his trousers and was slowly stroking it inches from my head.

Shaking my head in annoyance, I turned my attention from Jasmine's saturated vagina and scowled at Don. "You mind?"

Most likely, Don hadn't noticed that the head of his cock was about to graze my ear. The guy was quite the asshole, but he was a gentleman for the most part—an uneducated, slightly stupid one, but a gentleman just the same.

"Shit. Sorry, bro," he responded, moving a few inches away from me, waving his cock like it was saying 'good-bye.'

"Can I continue?" Jasmine lifted her head and gave us each a stare.

"Yeah, sorry, Jas," I responded.

"Sorry baby," Don chimed in after me.

Jasmine continued.

"Where was I?" she asked herself out loud, reclining and slipping as many fingers as she could into her cunt. "Oh yeah," she removed her hand from her crotch and let the juices drip onto her tongue, then swallowed. "So, anyway, the short of the story is, after we cut the fuck out of each other, the next step was adding some satanic rituals to the mix. Don's idea. He was the only reason I was even remotely okay with it. Of course, after seeing the results, I couldn't not be a believer!" She paused as she repositioned herself, bending over in my face.

"Are you telling me Satan made it so you all could...what? Just rip each other apart and grow new limbs?" Although my tone sounded smartassey, I was serious.

"Yeah, pretty much!" Jasmine responded.

Don waddled to the table's edge, kicked off his pants that were already bunched past his knees, then removed his boxers and flung them to a corner. He hopped up on the table next to Jasmine's face. Naturally, she put the tip of his penis in her mouth when it swung past her nose.

He leaned over and took hold of her buttocks with both hands. "She loves this!" He smiled at me, then hocked a loogy into Jasmine's spread ass cheeks. She let out a painful moan when he stuck his middle finger in her asshole over and over again. I figured he wanted me to be impressed or something; I had seen that done before.

"She likes a finger in the ass, gotcha!" I responded.

He just chuckled. "Nah, not that." Then, one by one, he shoved every finger into his wife's poop shoot until one hand was missing inside of her. Jasmine made sounds of pain but also of pleasure. Don laughed as he put his other hand down to Jasmine's mouth. She licked and sucked on his cock and his hand until both were dripping spit. Then he started to inch his spit-lubed hand in next to the hand already deep inside her ass.

The sounds coming from Jasmine's mouth became unbearable as Don wedged both hands inside her anus and began clapping. Whenever he lifted his hands out a little, gunk sloshed up around them and in between. Looking closer, I realized shit and blood was overflowing from Jasmine's buttocks as Don violently plunged inside her. When he thrust his hands deeper, her whole body jerked forward, landing her face first on the table. She tried to keep her balance, but her arms snapped at the elbows from the force of his thrust. She screamed in pain and then went back to moaning in pleasure.

"Jesus Christ!" I yelled. It was quite the situation. Usually, when someone was abusing a woman's anus in such a manner, one would be compelled to jump in and intervene—unless the woman had a smile going from ear to ear as Jasmine did at that moment.

"Yeah, she loves this, Chase!" Don spoke while still plowing away. "This is what we are talking about! Look at all this pain I am causing her!" he boasted, looking down at Jasmine as her body smacked repeatedly into the tabletop. "She's happy and laughing!" Her broken arms pulled further away from the skin, exposing bone and spurting blood.

Don quickly removed his hands from Jasmine's Hershey highway. She had become such dead weight that when he released himself from her, she smacked down hard enough for her breasts to make her bounce a little. This was when Jasmine lifted her head as much as she was able, opening her mouth wide enough to wrap around the head of his member. When she bit down, I wanted to puke.

Don released the worst shriek a man could scream. His usually deep voice raised to a much higher pitch. He gripped as hard as he could onto Jasmine's butt cheeks, gnashing his teeth as water poured from his eyes. Dark crimson smeared all over her round butt as he rubbed. He stood up on the edge of the table and grabbed his cock, which was spraying blood everywhere, including on me, unfortunately. I tried to run from it, but Don kept cutting me off wherever I ran.

Jasmine put her violated asshole down, causing her body to go flat. "Every few years, we need to make someone one of us to keep up the energy." She batted her eyelashes at me—a woman with two mangled arms with bones sticking out while her asshole poured multiple colors of liquids was winking at me. That was a strange image.

However, as weird as they were—and make no mistake, weird was putting it lightly—never in my life had anyone accepted me enough to include me in anything, not to mention something so unique and fucked up.

"We like you, Chase. We knew you would need some time before laying it out like we did." Don, still pouring blood from his headless cock, hopped up and down in excitement.

Jasmine tried to speak, but the head of Don's dick was in her mouth. She chewed faster and harder, finally swallowing the large, severed dickhead. "Come on, Chase, let's rip each other apart!"

A cold fear came over my body. This was where curiosity could kill a fucking cat. This was also where impulse took over.

Sighing deeply, I pulled my shirt over my head and slid my shorts down, launching them behind me. Then I leapt onto the table. I dug my face down into the mush of Jasmine's tormented pooper. Suddenly, the urge hit me to bite down as hard as possible. Her asshole had been stretched so wide that I had to sink my teeth in around the edges. The taste of fecal matter and lifeblood was like a combination of eating a penny and chewing on…well…a pile of shit.

Suddenly, I was struck in the face with Don's knuckles. Four teeth shot from my mouth, blood splashing along with them. I fell backwards. At first, I was confused, but when Don helped me up, I knew it was my turn. I recip-rocated with a slug to his forehead. He laughed as he fell backwards. As he had done for me, I helped him up.

"I'm glad you boys are having so much fun. Can I have a little fun, too?" Jasmine asked.

Don crawled to Jasmine on his knees and lifted her by her head. "Best head I ever had!" he joked.

"Very funny." She replied.

Don slammed her on the table and began beating her face in. That was hard to witness. She laughed and moaned. The whole time, teeth were shooting from her mouth, and facial bones were reconstructed. I watched as her new arm started to grow from behind the hanging part of her broken limb. It happened much quicker than in the video. As soon as one of her arms grew back completely, she punched Don in the face.

He replied by grabbing her and flipping her over. Picking up a knife that was on the table, Don planted a kiss on Jasmine and sliced downward into one of her breasts. It dangled from her side by a few strands of meat. He brought the knife down again, slicing her tit the rest of the way off.

Jasmine screamed, then grinned, mouthing the words "I love you" at Don before grabbing the shaft of his cock and aggressively stroking, causing the blood to run more freely. She held her mouth open, catching the rain of blood on her tongue and gulping it down as she continued.

Don tossed me the knife and nodded.

"Stick it in me, Chase! Make it fucking hurt!" Jasmine shouted.

The knife lay there in front of me, almost taunting me. Glancing up, I could see how excited Don was. Jasmine appeared to be pleased as well. I gripped that fucking knife and slammed it repeatedly into Jasmine's gut. Maroon poured from her mouth as she laughed.

"Slice my throat and fuck me!" Jasmine screamed.

I didn't give two shits about what Don thought. My cock was so hard, it was going inside her no matter what. I slid my hand over the place her breast used to be, soaked it with blood, then lubed my cock with it. Before shoving my erection into her, I raised the knife over my head. With two whisps of the blade, gashes were made across her neck. A look of pleasure and shock filled Jasmine's eyes as blood sprayed over my face and the front of her body.

My cock slid in without issue. I dropped the knife, then gripped her sides as I thrust myself inside of her. Her loud moan echoed throughout the house. Watching her remaining breast flop around as I fucked her, I needed to squeeze it. The way her stiff nipple felt in the palm of my hand was lovely. It wasn't something that happened to me often. My grip tightened as my nails dug deep into her fat fun bag.

Don had grabbed the knife at some point and crept up behind me, penetrating the middle of my back with it. The pain was terrible. It was like my back hurt but was also going numb. I fell to my side, crying.

"Keep fucking her! I know it hurts. It will only be bad for a few minutes," Don said, hopping down from the table. His dick was sprouting another head. It looked like a balloon filling up with water. He reached up and grabbed me by the back of my neck.

I tensed up. "Dude, I'm trying!" I had no choice. Regardless of the life-threatening stab wound in my back, wabbling and weak, I got to my knees. I was becoming weaker by the second. My cock was losing its stiffness.

"Fuck her before it's too late! You are going to fucking die!"

Those words were enough to light a fire under my ass. I stroked my cock while looking down at the fleshy mess that was Jasmine.

"That's right, baby, stroke that thing." She took her shaking hands and rubbed her love socket, spreading the lips open for me. Blood and cum dripped out.

My pecker could have broken concrete. UMPH! UMPH! UMPH! With those three thrusts, trying to go as far into Jasmine as I could, the flesh between her breasts started ripping open. I didn't stop fucking her. She screamed. The rip stretched down to her labia. I kept fucking.

Suddenly, my skin became like elastic and began connecting to Jasmine's flesh. The opening in the middle of her body spread, and blood oozed out. My body was being pulled into her. I screamed in misery, feeling like a piece of pulled pork. Inch by inch, I was disappearing inside of her.

Before I knew it, my body was engulfed in a sea of innards and multiple bodily fluids.

Then everything went black.

⸻ ☠ ⸻

It was like I was being reborn. All that I can remember from that experience was seeing bubbles of blood forming around my head—weird lights, dimming and flashing. I could hear Don and Jasmine speaking, but it was faint like I was underwater.

Before I knew it, I was lying in the shower, being hosed off by a scarred but beautiful Jasmine. She was still naked, revealing a scar going from between her breasts to her vagina. Don stood by, looking proud. He was still naked, occasionally grabbing at the semi-erection dangling between his legs.

After a few minutes, everything that had happened started to blur. I could only remember things in flashes. "What...what happened?" I asked, running a hand through my hair. A pink, slimy substance dripped from my fingers. When I shook my head, more goop flung from my hair.

"You're one of us now, Chase." Jasmine leaned down, placing her tit in my mouth. Like it was a habit, I cupped my mouth around her hard nipple and sucked. Warm liquid shot into my mouth.

"When he's done feeding, I think I am ready for a good, painful fuck!" Don laughed.

Standing up from the tub, I asked if I could be alone for a minute. I needed to get my head in the game. Jasmine nodded and walked out of the bathroom. Don winked and followed her.

⊷⊷•☠•⊷⊷

Now, here I stand, staring at myself in the mirror, looking into my own eyes, with images of my past dancing like a flip book. Sitting on the edge of the sink is a razor. Instinct tells me to grab it. I do. Fiercely digging the small blade across my face, blood dribbles from the cuts. I dig deeper into my skin. Pieces of flesh are falling from my face into the sink. I drop the razor and use my hands to grip the mangled chunks, pulling the meat from my forehead down. I scream as claret pours like a waterfall. This is who I am now—a fucking sadomasochist!

Time to remove Don's insides through his asshole.

MIDNIGHT AT THE DEAD DICK, FUCK-HOLE EMPORIUM

If you are reading this, that means you most likely made your way through the last tale of terror. Congratulations! I do hope you enjoyed yourself while reading it. Now, this next story makes the last one look like a booger.

This one was written for the Unveiling Nightmares anthology known as the Splatology. When I was first asked if I wanted to be a part of this anthology, I could not have said YES quickly enough!

Being told that I was able to write whatever my twisted fucking heart desired had me thinking; a Splatology needs to be extra gross with a slice of lemon and laughing gas! I wanted to write something that would fit all the tropes one would expect from an extreme/Splatterpunk story. This story has been told to stick out as one of the grossest stories some have read by me, and that makes me proud.

Make no mistake about it.

This is a story that is set out to cause a gross-out. Bring on the furries with 'tudes and the three women that are dying to give you a taste...this next one goes by the title, Midnight at the Dead Dick, Fuck-hole Emporium!

Earl Becker sat on the edge of the bed in the scuzzy motel room, taking the last few drags from his cigarette while chugging down the last drops from the silver can. To his left was a woman in her mid-twenties. Her body lay twisted, cattycorner on the bed, with her panties shoved in her mouth. A rope had been tightened around her neck.

While Earl was sitting in a booth enjoying a whiskey and Coke, the brunette stumbled into his arm, knocking his drink from his hand and bringing it to smash on the red-painted floor. The young woman turned to look. She was embarrassed at what her drunk ass had done, apologizing profusely. Earl saw no reason to be angry. He smiled, then offered the long-legged goddess with the hypnotizing chest a drink. She accepted. She accepted a lot—to the point of being trashed in Earl's motel room.

Earl had no real idea of what happened. Memories flashed through his mind, but not all together. The fact he'd killed her didn't bother him; it was that he couldn't remember doing it. This was his fourth kill. Usually, he wasn't drunk when he murdered. He wasn't even sure he'd wanted to kill this woman—it just happened.

Since this act of violence was random, Earl wasn't sure what his next step should be. There was the idea of digging into the trunk of his car for his usual tools and sawing her body up, stuffing the remains in baggies, and leaving them strewn throughout the county. The second idea was to leave her where she lay and get the fuck out of there before anyone suspected anything. He glanced at the clock. It was close to eleven PM. Surely, he could get out of dodge before anyone found the body. A grin spread across the bottom half of his face as a new idea occurred to him.

Earl walked out to his car to grab a bottle of bleach. He also wanted to take a quick view of the situation outside. There didn't appear to be anyone looming around. It was quiet as well. The only thing concerning him was the weather; the snow hadn't stopped for the past hour. It didn't show signs of slowing anytime soon, either.

After grabbing the bleach from his car, Earl hurried back into the room. With the snow coming down like it was, he didn't have much time to do what he wanted to do if he wanted to escape. He considered the upside of being snowed in with a dead body and all the necrophiliac fun he could have. Regardless, he preferred the idea of leaving.

Before making his grand getaway out into the winter weather, Earl grabbed the dead woman's ankles and pulled her body from the bed. She made a loud *THUD* as her purple-fleshed head smacked the floor, the rope still clinging to her neck.

Around the corner from the bed was the bathroom. Earl pulled the body across the floor. Her head dragged so hard against the filth-stained carpet that the panties he'd stuffed into her mouth to keep her from screaming were starting to fall from her dead pie-hole.

Earl grabbed her by her hair and threw her corpse violently into the tub. She landed with one leg draped over the tub's edge while the other stuck straight out. Her arms rested across her face. Looking down between her thighs, he saw a snapshot in his head of his face deep inside of her saturated cunt. He would have given her love socket another pounding or two if he had more time.

Instead of wetting his dick with the juices of the dead, Earl decided to do the next best thing. He'd find whatever he could to shove up inside this woman's perfectly shaved little pussy and asshole. It was a diabolical idea, indeed. No matter to him, it just sounded like fun. He wanted to leave some sign that a psychopath had been there. By the end of it, there would be no mistaking that a psychopath had been there.

Earl flipped the young woman's corpse and bent her body over. It was hard to keep her dead weight steady, but he figured it would be a more accessible position to fit as much as he could into her pleasure canals. It was no easy task. The pose left her head smooshed against the bathtub knobs, with the faucet shoved in her mouth. Earl smirked when he heard her jaw shatter.

When the struggle of positioning the body in the tub was figured out, Earl grabbed whatever he could think of. He placed two fingers into his mouth to get them wet, then shoved them into her rectum. He slid them in and out repeatedly.

He grabbed the plunger next to the toilet and rammed it as far as it would go, starting in her anal cavity and popping out of her throat. This also helped keep the cadaver in a doggy-style position, even with the top half of her body wanting to fall forward more. The sounds of her innards being penetrated, bursting within her stomach lining, made Earl's cock hard. He had to fight the urge to rub one out.

Earl slid one of his hands under the corpse, rubbing and probing her vagina. He couldn't tell if it was natural secretions or blood, but he could feel that she was wet—not too warm, but that didn't matter. A shampoo bottle sat on the edge of the tub. Earl reached over, quickly grabbing it, then spread her dead vagina wide enough to fit the cap of the bottle in. He gave one mighty push and managed to make the bottle disappear. This made him snicker.

The conditioner was next. Earl used four fingers on each hand to spread the hole wider, causing a gash. Blood trickled from the torn flesh. He stretched her once-pretty pussy as far as it would go. It split several areas as more blood trickled out.

It became easier to load the dead woman's cunt with a toothpaste container, a bar of soap from the sink, a pair of nail clippers, and finally ending with the scrub brush used to clean the toilet bowl. He crammed that brush in there, violently scrubbing the inner walls of her packed vagina, pushing everything he'd already buried deep inside her deeper.

Blood and feces oozed slowly from her backside, around the shaft of the plunger. Earl gagged. The smell was horrendous. He realized his job was done as viscous fluids poured from her many holes. It was time to get the fuck out of there.

Earl took the bleach, doused the body, and splashed it around the room. He didn't worry much about his actions coming back to bite him in the ass. As far as the motel went, he never checked in with the same name.

His exit from the motel had been smooth. But getting far away from the motel—not so smooth. The snow had picked up even more, and he found it hard to see if he was driving in the correct lane. It had only been ten minutes since he'd gotten back on the road when his tires began to slip and slide. He realized he wasn't going to be able to travel much further.

There was a glimmer of hope. A sign in big, red letters read: DEAD DICK'S ADULT VIDEO STORE AND MORE. Being the kind of guy Earl was, he figured it would be a suitable place to lay low. During this type of snowstorm, there weren't going to be cops giving much of a shit about pulling people over—especially at a porn store.

Earl followed the sign. His beat-up Sentra slid into every lane as he tried to make it safely into the video store parking lot. There weren't many cars in the parking lot, but there were a few—secluded enough to hide, enough cars to blend in.

It was midnight.

Rushing to ease into an icy spot, he hadn't noticed the building. Earl turned the engine off and raised his head. *Holy shit! This place is huge!* In front of him was what appeared to be a large strip mall turned late-night porn vendor. Every window had been blacked out and boarded up.

Walking up the dark walkway leading to the entrance door, Earl was taken back by the almost haunted house-looking sign draped across the wall next to it. The large tarp showed a figure resembling Satan, with sunglasses over his eyes and surrounded by cartoonish characters of devil women. Earl grinned.

The large glass door read ENTER. Earl tried. The door wouldn't budge. He scratched his head, then tried again. *What the hell is wrong with this fuckin' thing?*

BZZZ!

A sudden buzzing sound came from a speaker above the door. "Welcome to Dead Dicks! Are you ready to get off?" asked a sensual female voice. Earl smirked again.

"Sure." He replied, staring up at the speaker.

"That's good to know. There are many ways to make that happen within these walls. Try the door again, handsome."

The door handle made an unlatching sound, and it opened slightly. Earl grabbed the handle and pulled.

Upon walking through the door, he found himself in a small foyer. The windows had been blacked out. He looked around curiously, wondering what he was about to get into. Earl had always been the adventurous type, hence the whole killing people thing.

BZZZ!

A glass door slowly opened in front of him. As it opened, a bright light came from the other side. A woman walked up to him. She was wearing a leather skirt with a top to match. Tattoos covered both of her arms, which were crossed, projecting her massive mammaries. Her black hair was held back in a ponytail. A smile crossed her face while her brows went down to a point.

"Welcome to Dead Dick's!" said a man dressed in a tacky Hawaiian shirt who came out of nowhere.

Earl jumped back. "Damn, man. What a way to give a man a heart attack!" he exclaimed. The man just stood there, gnashing a fat cigar between his teeth. "Who are you exactly?"

The man stood there, gnashing a fat cigar between his teeth. "Well, isn't it obvious? I'm Dick!" He laughed.

"Yeah, I guess that would make sense," Earl remarked, walking further into the establishment. The mood outside the store was completely different from the vibe inside.

"Now, seeing as you are a first-time customer, we need to go over the menu system here." Dick was a very excited fellow.

"Menu system?" Earl asked, raising a brow.

"Well, of course! How the hell will we figure out what's going to fit your fancy otherwise?" Dick gave Earl the impression he may have been a car salesman at some point in his life. Earl would be shocked if he hadn't. "So, here's the deal!" he enthusiastically shouted, handing a laminated paper to Earl. "On that menu, you will find many exciting offers to ensure you have a wonderful time here! See what looks good to you, and if you mix and match, I'll give you a deal you can't refuse!"

Earl took his attention off the six-foot bald man to examine the paper in his hands. *It must be the worst menu I have ever seen.* He couldn't help but chuckle as he read the lists of what was offered. Some stuff wasn't that unusual, while every few lines, a curve ball would be thrown, and something off the wall would be listed. *Full Tug, full suck, missionary, doggystyle, glory-holes.* Earl took his free hand and combed his fingers through his sweaty hair. "So, this isn't a porn store?"

Dick's demeanor changed. "Oh, yeah. We do that, too." He reached down and flipped the menu that was in Earl's hand. There were titles upon titles of adult features to rent, buy, or watch there. Next to where it said WATCH IN STORE, it also read PUT ON A FLICK, SOMEONE'S SUCKING DICK. The phrase was off-putting. Earl knew what went on in those kinds of places. There were usually little rooms in the back where truck drivers and horny old men would cozy up to each other, watch porn and end up swallowing each other's meat sticks. Not a fiber of his being wanted any part of that shit.

"Go back to the front. I can tell you aren't thrilled by our 'movie list' and all its perks." Dick laughed, and a weird twinkle shone in his eye as Earl flipped the menu back over and surveyed the list of fantasies and kinks.

"What's the 'What the Hell? Special?'" Earl looked up from the menu to Dick, who was shaking his head, still gnashing the cigar, smiling from ear to ear.

"A bit of an adventurer, are you?" Dick asked, removing the cigar from his mouth, exhaling a cloud of smoke.

"I guess you could say that."

"Perfect! Many of our customers love this offer!" Dick placed an arm around Earl's shoulder. "You see... what's your name again?"

"Earl."

"Excellent! Earl!" He laughed. "Well, you see, Earl, this is exactly as it states. It's a 'what the hell?' scenario. We have taken the whole right side of the building and turned it into a mash-up of kinks. This is only for the strong. No weaklings allowed, if ya know what I mean. And I think you do." He smiled at the leather-clad woman; she smiled back.

"So what? I go back there and put my dick inside a bunch of glory holes without any idea of what's on the other side?" Earl wished his interest hadn't been piqued, but it had. There wasn't much to worry about. If this place were running some weird prostitution ring, they wouldn't want any attention brought to it. *The worst thing that might happen: a truck driver plays with my dick for a minute.* The thought made Earl want to puke. "When you say a mash-up of kinks, does that mean everything?"

"Well, there are glory holes, if you will, back there and..." he paused, smirked, then resumed, "Everything? Probably not. However, there's a fucking lot!"

"Jesus. There are women back there, right?"

Dick and the leather woman both cackled. "No worries. There are women back there, I assure you. But tuck in those insecurities. You gotta be open-minded!"

Still feeling the booze from earlier, his judgment was probably off more than it should have been when making such a decision. Part of him thought the whole thing was sketchy as fuck. But the desire to release the sexual mojo he'd built up, shoving all those items into the dead girl at the motel, outweighed his apprehension.

"Fuck it. How much?"

Dick seemed pleased. He walked over to the register sitting atop a glass case full of dildos and porno flicks. Taking his finger, he searched through a pricing list taped to the countertop. "Since you are a first-timer, I will take off a chunk, making the total only two hundred dollars, my friend."

"Why am I doing this?" Earl said out loud as he dug through his wallet, pulling out two one-hundred-dollar bills, and handing them over to dick, who popped open the register, shoved in the money, and pulled out a key.

"Here you are!" he said, handing the key to Earl.

Earl shook his head in disbelief at his strange reality. "Thanks. So where is the start of this sex gauntlet," he joked.

"Candy, take our friend here down to the start of the fun." Dick smiled while speaking. They wouldn't want any attention brought to it. *The worst thing that might happen: a truck driver plays with my dick for a minute.* The thought made Earl want to puke. "When you say a mash-up of kinks, does that mean everything?"

"Well, there are glory holes, if you will, back there and..." he paused, smirked, then resumed, "Everything? Probably not. However, there's a fucking lot!"

"Jesus. There are women back there, right?"

Dick and the leather woman both cackled. "No worries. There are women back there, I assure you. But tuck in those insecurities. You gotta be open-minded!"

Still feeling the booze from earlier, his judgment was probably off more than it should have been when making such a decision. Part of him thought the whole thing was sketchy as fuck. But the desire to release the sexual mojo he'd built up, shoving all those items into the dead girl at the motel, outweighed his apprehension.

"Fuck it. How much?"

Earl was amazed as he peaked through the doorway leading to the main showroom. It was huge. On one side of the room, the wall was covered in adult DVDs, and the other side was full of classic VHS titles from porn history. Earl noticed an old VHS copy of *Behind the Green Door*. *Holy shit! I haven't seen that one in years. Probably one of the creepiest fuck flicks from the seventies.*

In the middle of the lobby was an upscale-looking bar. Behind the counter, lights above and below illuminated the many bottles of expensive alcohol. A flat-screen television was mounted above the back wall amid the bottles. Earl guessed the screen must have been at least sixty inches. He looked at Candy, who giggled at his amazement. "Hey, how big is that TV?" he asked.

"I have no idea. If I had to guess, I'd say sixty," Candy answered as they approached the bar.

Knew it!

A chandelier hung from the ceiling above them. In front of them was a big black door. As they walked toward the door, Earl glanced at the whiskey bottles on the left side of the bar. "Is there any way I could get a drink or two before I go in?"

"Of course! We want you to feel good. Why do you think we have this here? A little liquid courage should enhance your journey." Candy walked behind the bar and grabbed a shiny glass. "What's your poison?"

Earl watched as Candy leaned down to get a scoop of ice. Her cleavage was a pleasant sight, and her leather top looked as if it were going to fall. He had his fingers crossed. "Whiskey on the rocks, please."

"Coming right up." Candy grabbed a bottle behind the bar and poured the brown liquid into the glass. Earl took the drink, gave the dangerously sexy woman a nod, and put it to his lips. In less than a minute, there was only ice remaining.

Earl belched. "That hit the spot!" he exclaimed, placing the glass on a metal coaster. He was startled when Dick's overly excited voice blared into his ear.

"Are you ready, Earl?" Dick said, then rubbed Earl's shoulders like he was a boxing coach or something.

"Hey, now!" Earl shrugged Dick's hands off. Dick jumped back, glaring into Earl's eyes.

"No need to get hasty, buddy! We are all here to have a good goddamn time! So, let's do that. Candy!" Dick snapped his fingers.

The black-haired beauty walked out from behind the bar, again grabbing Earl by the hand.

"Hey, I'm sorry, man. I get jumpy," Earl said as Candy led him to the big, black door.

Dick waved a hand, giving his best fake smile.

"So, how does this work exactly?" Earl asked as Candy placed a key into the hole above the doorknob.

"When you walk through this door. You are going to have a seat in front of the flat screen. Once a fetish is completed, a new door will unlock. Then, you move on… providing you can even keep going." Candy giggled. "That key you were given will get you into the last fetish room, as well as the exit." She turned the key, unlocked the door, and led him by the hand.

Earl got a foot inside the door when one last question occurred to him. He quickly looked back at Candy. "Hey, what happens if I can't finish a room?"

Candy blew him a kiss. "Don't pussy out, and you won't have to find out." Suddenly, her arms shot out, and she pushed Earl the rest of the way through the door.

The door locked behind Earl as he stared into the darkness. *Did I fuck up? I think I may have made a mistake.* Realizing he may be in over his head, he turned around and started to beat on the door. "Hey! I think I made a fuck up! Let me out!"

Dick's voice blared from a speaker. "Sorry, Earl. You see, I forgot to mention that all sales are final, and there are only two ways out, and backing out isn't one of them. Have fun!" There was a pause. "Now, go sit the fuck down!"

Earl turned his head and noticed a viewing seat in the corner and a flat-screen TV in front of it. He apprehensively crept over to the uncomfortable-looking pew. As he sat down, he looked at the screen. *The HD on this thing is unreal.* The screen was solid white. A tall woman wearing a long red dress with the sides cut up the thigh, showing off toned legs, came into view. The woman's hair appeared naturally red, with lipstick to match. *She has a whole Jessica Rabbit thing going on. I can dig this.*

The camera view panned over to show a naked man sitting on his knees with a ball gag in his mouth. Blood poured from a gash in his brow. His hands were cuffed behind his back, and he appeared to be crying.

The redhead looked into the camera. "If you are sitting in that seat, it means you must be new here. No one ever comes back twice."

"Fuck," Earl muttered.

"See this piece of shit?" the camera zoomed in on the man, only showing him from the neck up. She started talking to him like he was a dog. "Oh, look at you. You little piece of shit. Bad boy, you are. We are going to show the newbie what happens to pieces of shit." The camera zoomed back out, showing the woman in full view. She had her breasts out, tweaking her nipples with one hand and rubbing between her legs with the other.

This is about to get interesting. Earl wasn't expecting what came next. The camera zoomed in, only showing her tits and above. Her fingers pinched down hard on her nipples. She had a look of pleasure on her face—the type of pleasure brought on by pain.

Earl noticed that one of her hands was no longer playing with her fake tits. He could see she was doing something off-camera with her other hand. As the camera zoomed back out, Earl's eyes became huge as the shot revealed the woman was stroking a very stiff, massive, and engorged penis between her legs. The camera panned out more as she strutted toward the man.

The man tried to beg with the ball gag in his mouth, but it only came out as spitty mumbles. The red-headed woman walked out of view for a second, then returned and displayed the shiny, sharp-looking knife she held to the camera. The blade clearly wasn't made for hunting. It had a black handle covered in spikes, made to inflict pain.

The cameraman's hands got shaky, making it momentarily hard for Earl to see what was happening. When the picture became clear again, the camera was zoomed out enough to show that the redhead had ripped the ball gag from the man's mouth and was violently assaulting his throat. She plunged into the depths of his esophagus with her massive member. The man's eyes leaked water as they rolled into the back of his head. His handcuffed hands tensed as he tried to rip from his shackles. "You piece of shit!" She pulled her cock from his mouth, and saliva slapped to the floor below them.

Earl watched closely as the helpless man looked like he wanted to fall over. Every time the poor bastard got smacked in his face by that bitch's colossal cock, Earl couldn't help but laugh.

The redhead quickly turned her attention to the camera and winked. Then, while stroking aggressively with one hand, she raised the knife with the other and brought it down, slicing it into the top of the man's head. His body convulsed as blood splashed out. She removed the blade and ran it across his throat. Crimson sprayed her engorged member, and she let out a moan of pleasure as ropes of semen splashed the man's dying face. There was so much blood that Earl couldn't look away.

"Hey, Earl?" She spoke Earl's name.

"Shit."

Out of nowhere, a hidden compartment opened in the wall beneath the flat screen. The woman in red leapt out. Earl screamed as she grabbed him by the arms. From her face down, she was covered in red. "How funny is it, Earl? This could be you!" She laughed.

"Get the hell off me!" He shouted in her laughing face before pushing her onto the floor. Earl realized that the head of the man from the TV was still impaled around the woman's gargantuan meat pipe. "Jesus fuck!"

"Have fun, baby!" the redhead crawled back into the opening, then slammed it closed.

Earl heard the mechanical click as the next door—the gateway to whatever madness lay ahead—unlocked. *I don't want to keep going.* Earl stood and stared at the cracked door, waiting for him to open it all the way. "Hey! Dick! Let me out of here! Keep the fucking money. I don't want to be ripped apart by a six-foot transwoman! Okay?"

"Earl, you know I can't let you out." A soft-spoken Dick came over the speaker again. "Here's a little motivation for you." Another secret latch opened. An angry, muscular rottweiler stared Earl down. "If I were you, I'd get to moving, fuckface."

"Nice puppy." Earl shivered as the dog snarled at him. "Oh, come on!" The dog galloped towards him. The only place to run was through the next door. He bolted for the door and threw himself through, practically diving into the next room before slamming the door behind him.

"Oh boy," he muttered, looking around the new room he found himself in the middle of. There were no screens. This made Earl even more nervous. The walls were painted pink. Two more doors were on each side of the farthest wall. The lights weren't blinding but bright, like stage lights, shining down at the mystery doors.

Big fluffy couches lined the room. Earl thought the best idea was to hide behind one of them before whatever was behind those doors came out. Gripping the material of the giant couch, he thought it felt like a large marshmallow as he ducked down by its side.

When the doors unlocked, Earl couldn't see what was walking out. He sure as fuck heard the footsteps, though. Slowly, he lifted his head to peak from the side of the marshmallow couch. *Just when I think things couldn't get weirder...*

Standing on the other side of the couch, Earl saw two individuals dressed in animal costumes. One was a yellow rabbit, while the other was a blue bear. Both sported combat boots and bandanas around their fuzzy heads. *Great! Furry Rambos...*

The sight was disturbing enough to make Earl even more nervous. The rabbit held a steel mallet large enough to require both hands, and the bear was gripping a machete. *Well, this is truly a nightmare.*

Earl had been in many sticky situations, but this was a whole new ball game for him. He watched where the furies were stalking. He scaled the back of the couch, trying to remain hidden long enough to figure out his next move.

SLAM!

The yellow rabbit came over the top of the couch, slamming the mallet down on Earl's shoulder. Bone shattered as it made contact, and he fell face-first onto the floor.

"Jesus fucking Christ!" The injured side of his body pulsated with pain.

The furies laughed from under their masks.

The blue bear appeared above Earl and kicked him in the face before he could move out of reach, crashing him back to the floor. Blood shot from his nose as he went down. He glanced up in time to see a machete swing down at him. Rolling to the left, he narrowly avoided being chopped in half. The blade sparked as it hit the concrete floor with a loud CLANG.

The kick to the face caused Earl's vision to blur. He could tell the room's color had changed from pink to red. His body was lifted, and the bear tossed him into the corner.

"You fuck!" Earl cried out, spitting two teeth from his mouth. He could barely move but was able to turn in time to see both evil fucking furies lurking toward him. The top half of his body throbbed, and his face bled from multiple contusions. As bad as it hurt, Earl mustered his strength to lift himself off the floor.

"You ever been fucked by a furry before, Earl?" the rabbit asked, then launched the mallet in the terrified murderer's direction.

"Shit!" Earl shouted, almost taking a love tap from the giant mallet head. It smashed into the wall instead of his face. He was about to limp away when he saw a moment of opportunity. The bear was heading to the wall to retrieve his partner's weapon. Earl leapt at him, knocking them both onto the floor. With balled-up fists, he hammer-punched the disturbing character's chest. Earl relished the groans accompanying each blow as they issued from behind the fucker's mask.

The blue bear swatted at Earl but missed. Earl supposed the drawback of being a killer furry would be the difficulty the costume added to getting up and fighting back. Earl brought one last fist down, busting through the cheap mask. He grinned as he felt his knuckles smash the person's nose.

Glancing at the reflection in the broken eye of the bear mask, Earl saw the damn bunny raising the machete, about to bring it down onto his neck. When it came down, Earl moved, and the blade wedged into the bear's throat.

The bunny struggled to remove the machete from the almost-severed neck.

Earl raced to the mallet stuck in the wall. The bunny was preoccupied with sawing the machete blade from the bear's throat. Blood sprayed with every sawing motion. A final red geyser spewed from the bear's neck as the blade came free, and his head rolled to the side.

With both hands, Earl gripped the handle of the large mallet and pulled it from the wall. The timing was perfect. As he freed the mallet from the wall, the bunny swung the machete. The hammer side of the mallet knocked into the machete and sent it flying across the room.

The evil bunny panicked, unable to take two steps before being met with a blow to the back from Earl's mallet. As the bunny flew forward, the mask flew off. "Shit. Shit. Shit," a female screamed.

Creeping up to the bunny, Earl got a laugh, watching as the woman in the bunny suit tried to get up from the cold floor. Laying on her back was as far as she got. Then, it was like watching a turtle flipped on its shell. She looked up at him, grinning from ear to ear.

"What are you smiling about?" he asked.

"It doesn't matter what you do to me. You are going to suffer regardless." She laughed hysterically.

Earl shared her grin as he brought the mallet down on her face. A piece of her face chipped away with each repeated blow. By the end of it, her head was a bloody pile of brain matter, skull fragments, and mashed flesh.

The sound of a door unlocking caught his attention.

Moving to the right, he located the door, which was hidden by how the room was painted. The only way to tell a door existed was when it would unlatch and creak open a little.

Earl couldn't deny he was more nervous than he'd ever been before he started his trek through the kink factory. Hell, the only thing he'd worried about before was being raped by a dude or something. But judging by what he'd already experienced in the brief time he had been there, he knew he was bound to get fucked in more ways than he could imagine.

Dragging the mallet behind him, he slowly approached the door.

The loudspeaker was flipped on again. "Ummm, sorry, bud. No weapons can be taken to the next room."

Earl shook his head, trying to disobey.

"Wouldn't do that if I were you," Dick said.

"Fuck you!" Earl shouted, putting his free hand on the doorknob.

TZZZ!

A shock came from the knob, stunning his entire body. The mallet dropped from his hand. He let go of the doorknob.

"Now. Enter. Play nice, asshole." Even though Dick maintained a chipper tone, there was irritation hidden between words.

Not thrilled at having to move on without any protection, Earl grabbed the doorknob again. This time, nothing shocking happened. The door pulled back smoothly as he moved to the next room.

This room was smaller than the last. Where the previous room was as big as a two-car garage, this room was the size of a master bedroom with high ceilings. Like the main lobby, a chandelier hung from above. It may have resembled a nice bedroom, but there was no bed. In the middle of the room were three stirrups. The sight piqued his interest, knowing it couldn't be anything so delightful.

A door in the corner of the purple-painted room opened. If it were someone's bedroom, it would be where a walk-in closet or a bathroom would usually be. Earl's eyes grew large as he watched three beautiful women walk out, each wearing only bikini bottoms.

The first woman to walk out looked to be in her early twenties, with short blonde hair, porcelain skin, and the cutest little A cups Earl had ever seen. It was drafty in the room, colder than the others had been, and each woman's rock-hard nipples pointing in front of them confirmed the temperature.

The woman who walked out after the blonde was a little thicker in size. Dark, wavy hair hung down past her shoulders. Earl wasn't sure of the size of her breasts, but he knew they were bigger than double D's. She gave him a wink as she headed to the stirrups.

The final woman to walk through the door didn't appear as full of life as the other two. They both were smiling and shaking their tits around, but not this one. Her hair was in braids, and the color was a mess. It was like she had dyed her hair too many colors at once. The tattoos on her arms, showing images of moon signs, pot leaves, and Grateful Dead bears, led Earl to believe she was some kind of hippie. Like the other two, she was also a gorgeous woman. However, she looked ill. Her skin was sickly pale—almost gray.

Each woman stood next to a stirrup.

The loudspeaker clicked on again. "I can see you are a little more at ease with this one so far, Earl. Well, I just wanted to come on and let you know that you shouldn't put your guard down just yet." Dick laughed. "Ladies, please take your positions."

Each woman slid off their bottoms, tossing them to the side. Earl grinned like a kid finding a Playboy for the first time. He couldn't help but be visually stimulated. The thicker woman had a thin layer of hair on her pubis (the landing strip), and the blonde was smoothly shaved. The hippy, however, showcased an unruly, unkempt bush.

When the three women climbed up, placed their legs into the stirrups, and spread them, Earl shuddered in his skin. Nothing appeared too concerning when the Thicker, dark-headed beauty spread her legs. He glanced over at the blonde, noticing a string dangling from her fuck socket. *That's promising,* he thought to himself, shaking his head. There was something physically wrong with the hippy chick, though. She was shaking. Her eyes rolled back in her head.

"Hey Earl! You like eating pussy?" Dick hollered over the loudspeaker.

Out of nowhere, Earl was grabbed by two individuals and then received a swift kick to the back of the leg. He fell to his knees. As he was picked back up, he saw the two people detaining him were muscle-bound men. They were dressed in leather with leather masks to match. Both had zippers over their mouths.

The men dragged Earl to the stirrups where the thicker girl was spread out. One man shoved Earl's head down into the woman's crotch. He gave it a quick look and still couldn't find anything wrong with her pretty pussy.

"Eat it!" the masked man holding his head down commanded.

When Earl was about to oblige, Dick's voice echoed from the speakers once again. "Meredith, why don't you spread that pretty peach open more."

The woman did as she was directed. She smirked at Earl as she used her fingers to spread her sex wider. A flood of white fluid gargled out of her. "Ever wonder what a twenty-man creampie looks like close up?"

Earl swung his arms around violently, trying to pop one of the masked men in the face—no such luck. The men were bigger, not to mention much stronger than he was. The man holding him by the neck squeezed tighter, sinking his fingers deep. Earl already knew what was coming next.

The big-handed man shoved Earl's mouth into the river of semen flowing from Meredith's vagina. He gagged as he felt the warm goo touch his lips.

"Eat it!" the other masked man demanded, grabbing him by the face and prying open his mouth. "Lap it up, big man!"

After being physically forced to slurp up most of what was pouring from between those thick thighs, the men let go of Earl, allowing him to fall to his knees and puke up a belly full of man-snot. He wiped his face with his sleeves. Then it was back to work.

The blonde leaned back, a warm smile running from ear to ear. Her eyebrows came down to a point. She ran her fingers down her naked breasts, leading them down to the clean-shaven pink paradise between her legs. Earl smiled at her, face still dripping slime, forgetting the atrocity he'd just been through. Then he remembered the string he'd noticed dangling from inside her shaven haven.

Following her hands with his eyes, he remembered why he was concerned about this one. Her nimble fingers swiftly plucked the string and yanked out a blood-soaked tampon. One of the masked men gripped a chunk of Earl's hair, pulling him closer. The blonde grabbed him by the jaw, pried his mouth open, and shoved the saturated tampon down his throat.

Earl gagged, watching in horror as she reached down again, pulling out another soaked tampon. It looked more decrepit than the previous one—like it had been marinading a while.

Earl gagged again, coughing up the first tampon from his throat. However, before he was able to spit it out, the blonde shoved the browner-looking tampon into his mouth, pushing the first one back down his throat. He could feel the vomit rising from his stomach. This routine went on for another two minutes. One after another, the blonde pulled out tampons like a clown with colored handkerchiefs, shoving every last one of them into Earl's mouth.

Both men standing behind him shared a laugh when they threw Earl to the ground to puke once again. Holding himself up by his hands and knees, an overload of used tampons fell from his mouth. A few didn't want to come out, and if the vomit didn't push them out, he retrieved them with his fingers, causing more vomit to spew from his lips.

In short order, the men lifted him again. This time, he found himself in front of the sickly-looking hippy with the killer bush. There was something wrong with her. She lay there moaning with displeasure.

"For fuck's sake! Don't make me do it!" Earl screamed, seeing that hidden beyond the valley of hair was a very infected-looking vagina.

Earl fought hard, making it difficult for the men to keep a hold of him. One grabbed one arm while the other did the same on the other side. They twisted his arms, forcing him into a bent-over position. In his history with women, he had been with some questionable and downright disgusting women. But nothing compared to what his eyes beheld. This giant gash of a love socket was green with infection, dripping odorous pus, and writhing with maggot-looking worms. Tiny insects milled about on the layer of scabs crusting her thighs.

Earl's gag reflex returned with a vengeance.

"Last one, shithead! You're almost free!"

"Goddammit," Earl muttered, shying away from the gross gash.

The hands on his face and neck were too strong. As they forced him to place his open mouth over the wet, worm playground, the hippy began convulsing—then suddenly stopped—*as if things couldn't get worse!* The feeling of his lips resting around the open hole while bugs wandered around on his tongue was the most horrifying and disgusting thing he'd ever experienced. Then something started to fill up his mouth.

"Swallow it!" the masked man on the right demanded.

The taste was like snot pouring down his throat, and the smell was pungent. Earl jerked his body, trying to get free, and failed. However, as the men struggled to keep him tame, they lost some of their grip. He was able to remove his mouth from the infection zone, turn around, and spit the neon green substance into one of the masked men's eyes.

Earl was quickly met with a punch to the face, knocking him away from the men. He looked at the hippy girl. She was dead. Worms fell from her spread legs onto the floor, which was already covered in a cocktail of human fluids.

The masked men charged at him.

"Stop! You know what? Let him go on to the next round. This one leads to the end, you sick fuck!" Dick's cackles could be heard throughout the entire building.

The masked men stopped, turned to their left side, and marched out of the room. There was no unlocking sound, but the next door was noticeable when a spotlight turned on above it. Remembering the key he'd been given, he pulled it from his pocket and staggered to the door.

By this point, Earl was disoriented. The intoxication he'd entered with had become a hangover. He'd been beaten and had his mouth raped. It was time to get the fuck out of there.

The key fit as he slid it into the hole. The lock turned. Excitedly, he swung the door open, hoping to see an EXIT sign shining in his face. His expectations were too high.

In front of Earl were two ways to go. On one side was a green wall with multiple holes in it. The other way led to a giant black metal door. A strong odor lingered from the door's direction. He looked in the room with the holes. There didn't seem to be any way out from there.

Making a split-second decision, he ran to the black door. It looked more like the door of a bank vault. There was no doorknob, just a big metal wheel that needed to be turned.

Earl hoped to open the door and find an easy kink waiting for him as a reward for all his hard work getting to the end. Such was not the case. It took all his energy, but he got that big bastard of a door open. The smell burned his nostrils. The sight before him was something he never expected.

It was a pool. There was no telling how deep it was. It was full—but not full of water. It was shit! Human feces, no doubt. But that wasn't all... Chunks of human flesh and limbs floated in the bog. Earl noticed the head of the guy who got face fucked at the beginning of the whole nightmare.

Being so grossed out, he missed the guy dressed in leather standing in the corner, lathering himself up in fecal matter. "Come on in. It's so warm and squishy. You want out, don't you?"

The words made goosebumps spread across Earl's skin. The way out was somewhere in that room.

Earl had his nose pinched, but the fumes still managed to invade his sinuses. "Fuck this! I am not swimming in shit, Dick!" Using both hands, he slammed the black metal door.

Dick didn't say a word, just laughed over the speaker.

Earl stomped to the wall filled with holes. *Maybe one of these holes would open a way out. What if this is just a choice of what's a worse way to be free?* In the middle of the wall was a note. All it said was PICK A HOLE. It could only mean one thing.

Without hesitation, he pulled his cock from his pants and plopped it into the closest hole. The feeling of wanting to collapse rushed over him. His head felt dizzy. As he stood with his flaccid penis dangling within the green wall, something started playing with it. Fingernails combed the shaft back and forth. It felt nice—relaxing even... until it was sucked into someone's mouth and bitten.

A wail of torment escaped Earl's mouth as he pulled back, seeing his pathetic meat stick was no longer where it was supposed to be. All he had now was a bloody stump, which bled like a stuck pig, soaking the wall in crimson.

He started crying and fell to his knees, inadvertently placing his face in front of one of the holes. As soon as he did, the end of a double-barrel shotgun poked through, emptying both barrels into his face. The explosion of Earl's head sent a splatter in every direction. Brains, blood, and flesh painted the ceiling and floor.

"Okay, people. We got another sick fuck moron coming in. Dump this pile of shit where shit goes. I'm sure the septic man would love a new plaything!"

ABOUT THE AUTHOR

Chuck Nasty came from the womb with his middle fingers up!

He may be from the blue grass state, however, make no mistake about it, he's here to make sure the red still flows.

When he isn't working on writing projects, he plays drums and does main vocals for the two piece sludge band Bastard Sons of a Judas Goat and does the podcast thing on: Nasty Nation, video store clerks podcast and Graveyard Talk.

The authors that inspire Chuck are: Stephen King, Clive Barker, Edward Lee, RL Stine, Chuck Palahniuk and Hunter S Thompson.